W9-BGY-941

Originally published as *Fred is druk* in Belgium and Holland by Clavis Uitgeverij, Hasselt – Amsterdam, 2017 English translation from the Dutch by Clavis Publishing Inc., New York

Visit us on the Web at www.clavisbooks.com.

Fred Wants to Play written by Janna de Lathouder and illustrated by Anne Schneider

ISBN 978-1-60537-388-1

This book was printed in March 2018 at DENONA d.o.o., Zagreb, Marina Getaldica 1, Croatia.

First Edition
10 9 8 7 6 5 4 3 2 1

Clavis Publishing supports the First Amendment and celebrates the right to read.

Written by Janna de Lathouder
Illustrated by Anne Schneider

Fred Wants to Play

NEW YORK

It's quiet time, but Fred has trouble keeping still.
He feels something bouncing inside him.

FLING FLANG FLONG
PLUNG PLANG PLONG

When Fred has that feeling,
there's only one thing he really wants to do . . .

PLAY!

But the other fish don't want Fred to play with them.

"You have to calm down."
"Yes, try to calm down."
"You are too wild."

So Fred tries to calm down.
He sits on his tentacles, but that doesn't help.
Maybe if he ties himself in knots . . . ?
FLING FLANG FLONG
PLUNG PLANG PLONG
But the bouncy feeling keeps coming.
He feels like he is filled with all the colors of the rainbow.
Fred tries to keep the feeling inside.
He closes his eyes and squeezes tight.

But then . . .
Oh no!

Fred can't control himself anymore!
The bouncy feeling bursts out
and flies in all directions.

FLING FLANG FLONG
PLUNG PLANG PLONG

"Watch out!" the others cry as they swim away.

"There you go again," the sawfish say.
"Why can't you keep still like the other fish?"
"If you can't keep still, you can't stay here."

Sadly, Fred swims away.

Fred swims and swims.
All of his colorful feelings are gone.
He just feels sad . . .

. . . and alone.
Very alone.

What's that?
Fred sees a big shell.
Whose could it be?
Fred knocks. There's no answer.
Fred knocks again.
What a fun sound!
Fred feels the bouncy feeling coming back.
He knocks and knocks again. No one is around to hear him or get mad at him.

KNOCK KNOCK
KNOCKETY KNOCK
KNOCK KNOCK
KNICK KNACK KNOCK

Suddenly the shell opens and . . . snap!
One of Fred's tentacles is trapped!
"Ouch!" Fred calls. "Ow, ow! Let go!"

"Oops! Sorry!" comes a voice from inside the shell.
"I wasn't trying to hurt you. I was just playing."

"You call that playing?" Fred squeaks. "Let me go, please!"
"I can't help it," said the voice.
"Sometimes I feel a bouncy feeling inside of me and I just have to play!"

The shell opens and Fred's tentacle is free.

Hey—what did he say?
A bouncy feeling?
Fred doesn't believe his ears.

"Hey, I have that bouncy feeling too!" Fred calls enthusiastically.
The shell opens a little bit.
"Really? I thought I was the only one in the entire ocean!" says the voice.
"I thought so too!" Fred answers.

"My name's Fred. What's yours?"
"I'm Scott. And I'm so happy to meet you!"
Fred and Scott began to talk. They talked about the colors
they get when they try to hold in the bouncing.
And about how no one wants to play with them.
And about feeling all alone in the big ocean.

Fred and Scott think of a plan.
A real bouncy plan.
"Let's go!" Fred says happily.

"Yoo-hoo, I'm back!" Fred calls.
But no one is around.
"Where is everyone?" Scott asks.

"They will come out when they see what we have planned," Fred says.
"Let's get this party started," agrees Scott.
Scott floats down to the ocean floor and Fred swims down with him.

From inside his shell, Scott begins to knock.

KNOCK KNOCK
KNOCKETY KNOCK KNOCK KNOCK
KNICK KNACK KNOCK

Then Fred joins in.
He dances along to the beat, and his colorful feelings bounce out.

FLING FLANG FLONG
PLUNG PLANG PLONG

The seahorses, sawfish, and all the other fish are getting curious.
“What’s that nice sound?” the sawfish ask.

The other fish gather 'round.
Fred and Scott are having so much fun making music.
Colorful sounds are bouncing everywhere.

Everyone joins in.
"It was so quiet when you were away," the sawfish tell Fred.
"Too quiet!" the other fish agree.

What a happy place!
"Let's play!" says Fred.
PLUNG PLANG PLONG
Hooray!